# Clarence the Nosey Dragon

by Diane Jackman

Illustrated by Angela Mills

Brimax • Newmarket • England

Clarence is a very nosey dragon. He pokes his long, green nose into everything.

"No good will come of this," warns his aunt. "One day you will end up in a lot of trouble."

Clarence takes no notice of his aunt's words.

"I am not really nosey," he says. "I am what you call interested in things."

He opens his aunt's bag when she comes home from shopping. He finds the train set she has bought him for his birthday. He looks into his aunt's work-box. He finds the scarf she is knitting for him. He peeps into the cake tin in the cupboard. He finds his birthday cake.

"Why do you do it, Clarence?" asks his aunt. "Now you have spoiled all your surprises."
But Clarence cannot stop. He lifts the lids of boxes. He unties the tops of sacks. He opens cupboards and pulls out drawers.
"I am only interested in things," he says. But really he is the nosiest dragon that has ever lived.

One morning Clarence is on his way to school. He sees a little pile of white powder on the path. Then another, and another. He follows the trail of powder until he comes to a signpost. To the left is the way to school. To the right, the trail of powder trickles on. Clarence makes up his mind. He goes right.

On and on the trail leads. Up hills and down into valleys. Clarence does not give up. He wants to know what lays at the end of the trail. He follows it along the road, across a bridge, and up to the door of a windmill. Clarence does not stop to think. He pulls open the door and goes in.

It is quite dark inside the
mill. Clarence pokes his nose into
every corner. He finds wheels,
chains and levers. He finds
sacks of corn and sacks of
flour. He finds mice hiding in
the corn bin.
"What an interesting place,"
says Clarence. "Now I wonder
what this does." He pulls hard
on a shiny brass lever.

He soon finds out. Above his head the sails of the windmill turn. The big mill-stone moves slowly round. Clouds of flour begin to fill the air. A strong gust of wind blows through the windmill as the sails turn round. The door slams shut. Clarence pulls as hard as he can, but it will not open.

"Oh," wails Clarence. "If only I had not been so nosey. . . I mean interested."

He tries to climb out of the window, but it is too small.

It is also a long way down to the ground.

"I will have to call for help. Although I will end up in trouble, just like my aunt always says." He shivers at the thought of his aunt.

The farmers are puzzled. The windmill's sails are turning, but today is the day the miller always goes in to town. Clarence puts his head out of the window. "Help! Help!" he calls. Now, when dragons are frightened, they breathe fire. So the farmers suddenly see flames leaping out of the windmill window.

"Fire!" they shout. "Fetch some water!"

The farmers begin to run through the streets with buckets of water. Some even have hoses. They throw the water over the windmill. A jet of water hits Clarence at the window. He pulls his head inside quickly. He is soaking wet.

"They must stop," says Clarence.
"The water will spoil the
miller's flour." He shouts out
of the window again.
"Stop! Stop!" But flames shoot
out of his mouth. Another jet
of water sprays over him. He
runs upstairs to a higher
window. The farmers think the
fire has spread. Again they turn
their hoses on Clarence.

Clarence sits on a flour-sack. He does not know what to do next. "I think the fire is out," says one of the farmers. "Time to break down the door."
Inside they find a mountain of sticky, soggy flour and a wet, unhappy dragon. Water runs off him at every corner.
At that moment the miller comes down the street, home from the town.

Clarence is in deep trouble.
The farmers are cross. The
miller is very cross. His aunt
is very, very cross!
''I always said you would end
up in trouble,'' she scolds.
''And I was right!''
Clarence sneezes unhappily.
''I am very sorry,'' he says.
''I promise not to be quite
so nosey in the future!''

# Say these words again.

nosey          cupboard

warns          surprises

notice         drawers

interested     trickles

shopping       window

birthday       shiny

knitting       shivers